LAURA LIPPMAN is the award-winning writer of more than twenty crime-fiction novels. She lives in Baltimore and New Orleans with her husband, David Simon, and her very smart daughter, Georgia Rae.

KATE SAMWORTH is a painter and illustrator from Maryland. Her paintings and prints have been exhibited around the country and abroad and can be found in the collections of the Kyoto Municipal Museum of Art, the Woodmere Art Museum, the Fundación Lolita Rubial (Uruguay), and the New Orleans Academy of Fine Arts. Her first book, *Aviary Wonders Inc.*, won the Kirkus Prize for Young Readers in 2014.

Artwork photographed by John von Pamer and Brennan Cavanaugh

Published by Akashic Books
Words ©2018 Laura Lippman
Illustrations ©2018 Kate Samworth

ISBN: 978-1-61775-661-0
Library of Congress Control Number: 2018931286

Printed in China
First printing

Black Sheep/Akashic Books
Brooklyn, New York, USA
Ballydehob, Co. Cork, Ireland
Twitter: @AkashicBooks
Facebook: AkashicBooks
E-mail: info@akashicbooks.com
Website: www.akashicbooks.com

LIZA JANE & the DRAGON

by LAURA LIPPMAN

illustrated by KATE SAMWORTH

Liza Jane was a lucky girl. Her parents told her so every day.

She had a bed with a canopy, a fish named Swimmer, and she was allowed to use the remote control as long as there was a grown-up in the room. Her bedroom ceiling had stars that glowed in the dark and it looked like the real night sky because her dad knew everything about stars. She had to wear a uniform to school, but she had a dress-up box with six princess dresses and all her mother's old shoes.

On Friday nights, her mother put a cloth on the floor and they had pizza picnics while watching a movie that Liza Jane picked. She was lucky.

Her parents told her so every day.

Yet: People didn't listen to her.

People interrupted her.

People didn't care about her feelings.

And by "people"—we mean her parents. Sometimes teachers.

Even, every now and then, her best friend. But mostly her parents.

So Liza Jane fired them.

She then had to find new parents.

She asked her teddy bear, but he was too soft.

She asked her fish,
but Swimmer moved
his mouth, yet said
nothing.

Finally, she put up signs around the neighborhood.

A dragon came to the door.

"I can do both jobs," the dragon said.

"You have to listen to me. Pay attention to my feelings. Tell people not to make me angry."

"I can do that."

"And you must never interr—"

"No problemo," said the dragon.

The first night, she showed the dragon how to order pizza for dinner, although it wasn't Friday.

The pizza delivery person was very late and the pizza was cold and it had pepperoni on both sides when Liza Jane said only half pepperoni, so she cried a little.

And the dragon set the pizza delivery person's car on fire.

"That's not very nice," Liza Jane said.
"Hey," the dragon said, "I'm a dragon."

The next day, they were late for school because the dragon wasn't very good at brushing hair.

"I can't hold the hairbrush in my claws," the dragon said.
"I'm a dragon."

The lady at the front desk said: "You'll need a late pass."

Liza Jane said: "It's only a minute past 8 a.m. —"

"You know the rules."

"I hate rules," Liza Jane said. "And you interrupted me."

So the dragon set the front desk on fire.

"You can't set fires
in the school building,"
Liza Jane said.

"Hey," the dragon said, "I'm a dragon."

That became life with the dragon, every day. Pizza, because the dragon couldn't cook. Knotty hair, because the dragon couldn't hold a brush. Getting to school late, because the dragon couldn't tell time.

And if anything made Liza Jane mad or frustrated, the dragon set it on fire. Such as the remote control. And her homework. And even the canopy on her canopy bed. Whenever Liza Jane tried to tell the dragon to stop or take it easy, he said:

"Hey, I'm a dragon."

Soon the walls were scorched.

And the rugs. And even the top of her teddy bear's head.

Yet: He listened to her. He never interrupted.

If she got mad, he got mad. Which felt good.

Except for the everything-being-burned part.

There came a day when the house had holes in the roof and the walls. And the pizza delivery person began leaving the pizza on the doorstep and driving away really fast.

Liza Jane was sick of pizza, anyway.

Her teacher didn't want to tell her when she'd made mistakes on her homework, because what if she got mad?

Kids in her class didn't want to play with her because the dragon was always standing by, glaring at them.

"Maybe you could be a little nicer," Liza Jane said to the dragon.

"Hey," said the dragon, "I'm a dragon."

After two weeks, or maybe it was six months, or maybe it was four years, Liza Jane said: "I think you should go and I should get my parents back."

The dragon said: "I love you. I did what you asked me to do. It's just that~"

"I know," Liza Jane said. "You're a dragon."

"I hate it when you interrupt me."

Liza Jane thanked the dragon for its service
and put up ads in the neighborhood.

Her mom and dad were the first ones to apply.
She hired them.

She tells them every day how lucky they are.